For Will and Elle,

Only as far as you seek,
Can you go...
Only as much as you dream,
Can you be!

Dennett

Ned The Nuclear Submarine

Written and Illustrated by

Demetri Capetanopoulos

Book Design & Production: Columbus Publishing Lab
www.ColumbusPublishingLab.com

Copyright © 2018 by Demetri Capetanopoulos

LCCN: 2018963081
Paperback ISBN: 978-1-63337-238-2
Hardcover ISBN: 978-1-63337-239-9
E-book ISBN: 978-1-63337-240-5

Printed in the United States of America
1 3 5 7 9 10 8 6 4 2

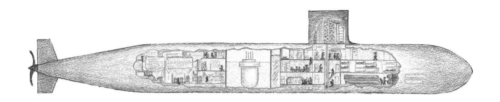

Dedicated to Leo
and to courageous souls everywhere
who boldly go...

Twenty years from now you will be more disappointed by the things you didn't do than the ones you did do. So throw off your bowlines. Sail away from safe harbor. Catch the trade winds in your sails. Explore. Dream. Discover.

—Mark Twain

Ned was a nuclear submarine,
built of high-strength steel,

born of a thousand workmen,
by the river where they laid his keel.

They filled him inside with their skill and their pride,
in addition to pipes, tanks, and wires.

Made to sail all the seas, just as long as you please,
fueled by his nuclear fires.

There were speeches of plans and crowds in the stands,
who watched him slip into the river.

But Ned didn't feel bold, nor particularly cold,
nonetheless he gave a small shiver.

For as he considered his upcoming voyage,
and what all the people expected,

he felt unsure, untested, and unprepared,
his worries growing the more he reflected.

The tugboats who nudged him to his new home base,
were hardly any consolation.

They couldn't imagine venturing out to face,
what lay beyond the naval station.

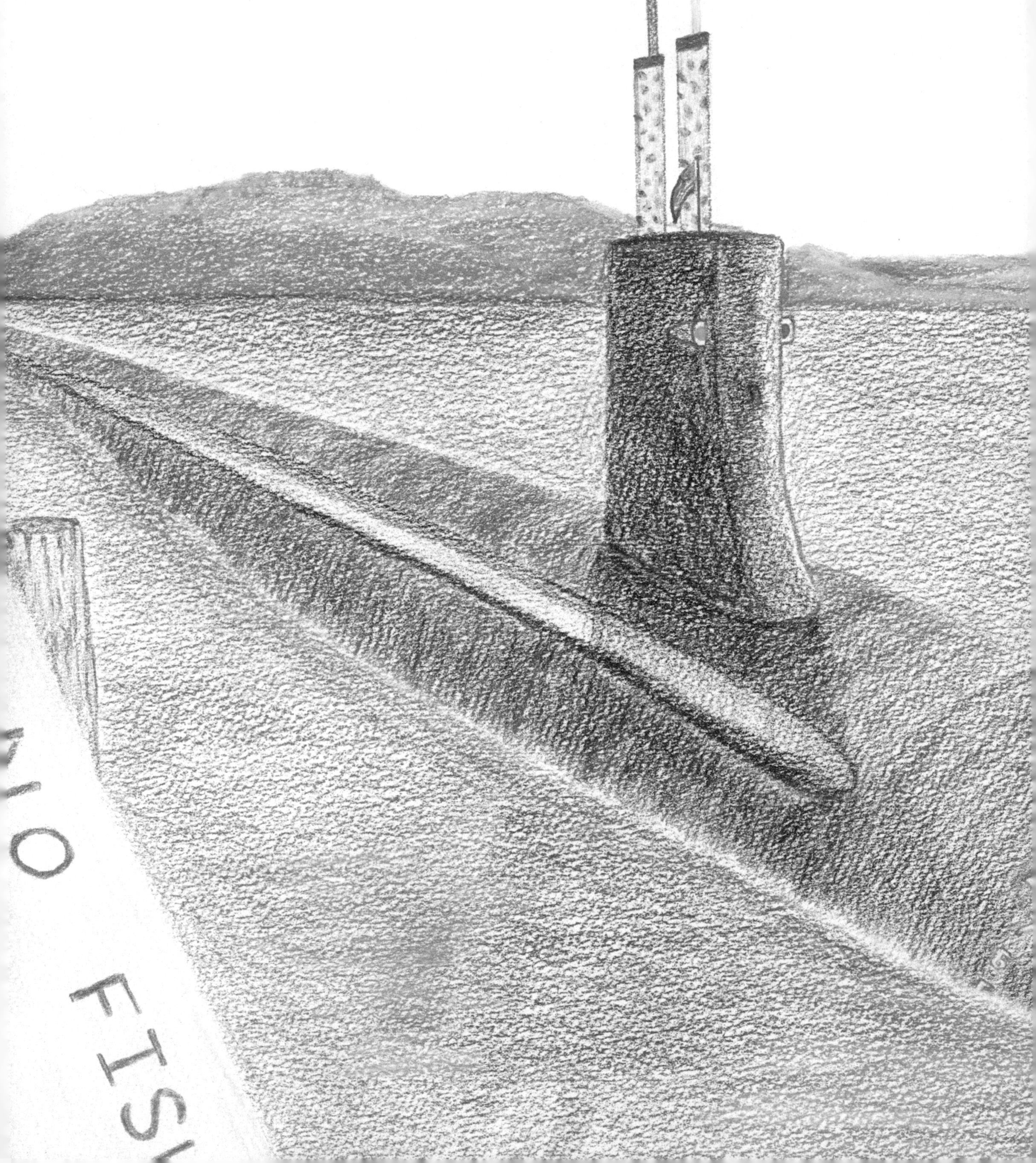

They wouldn't go, so they couldn't know,
and they didn't intend to be mean.

But they filled his head with all kinds of dread,
of things they never had seen.

They spoke of bottomless seas, and getting lost,
and where the earth might end,

suggesting monsters might even lurk,
beyond the river's bend.

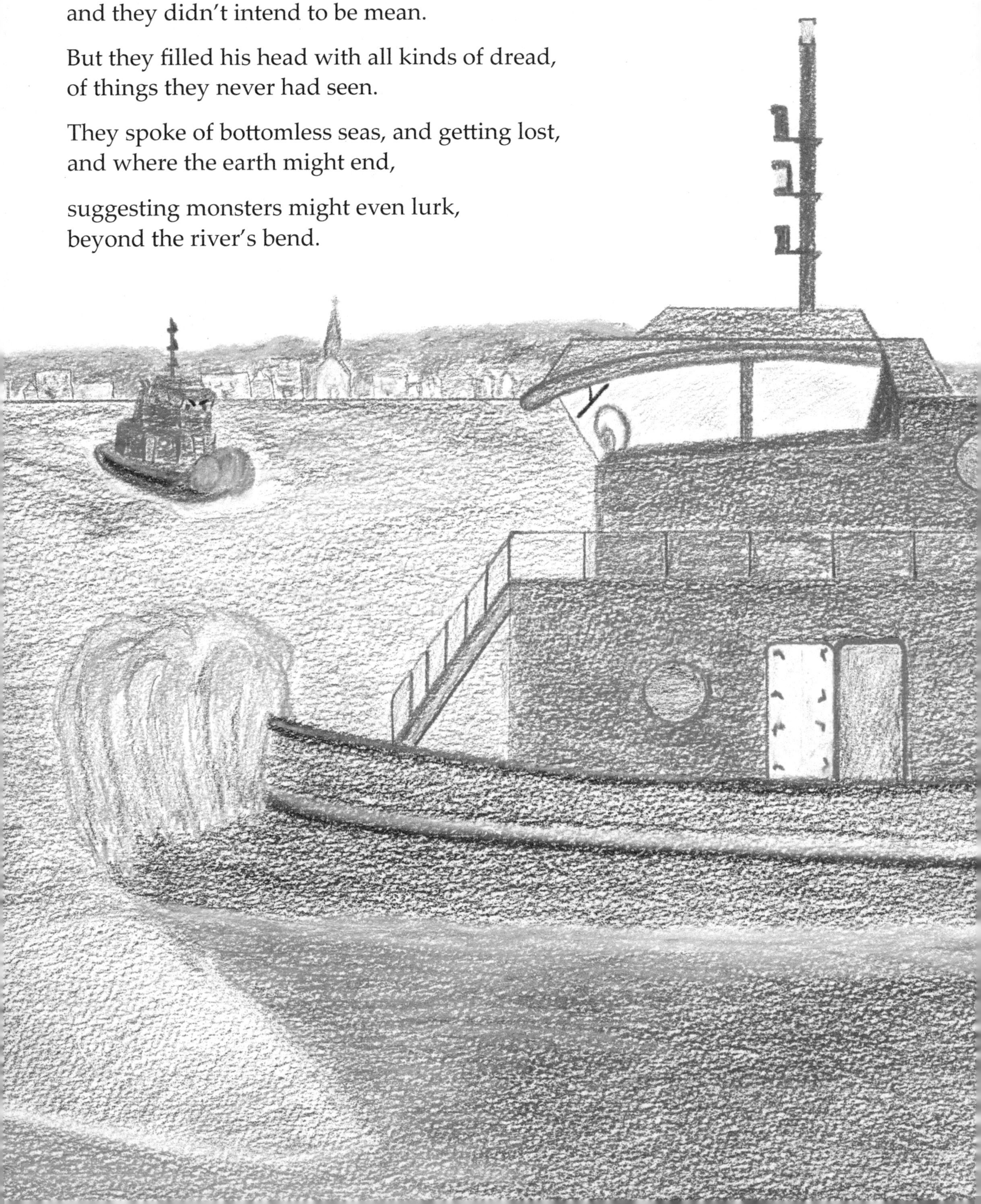

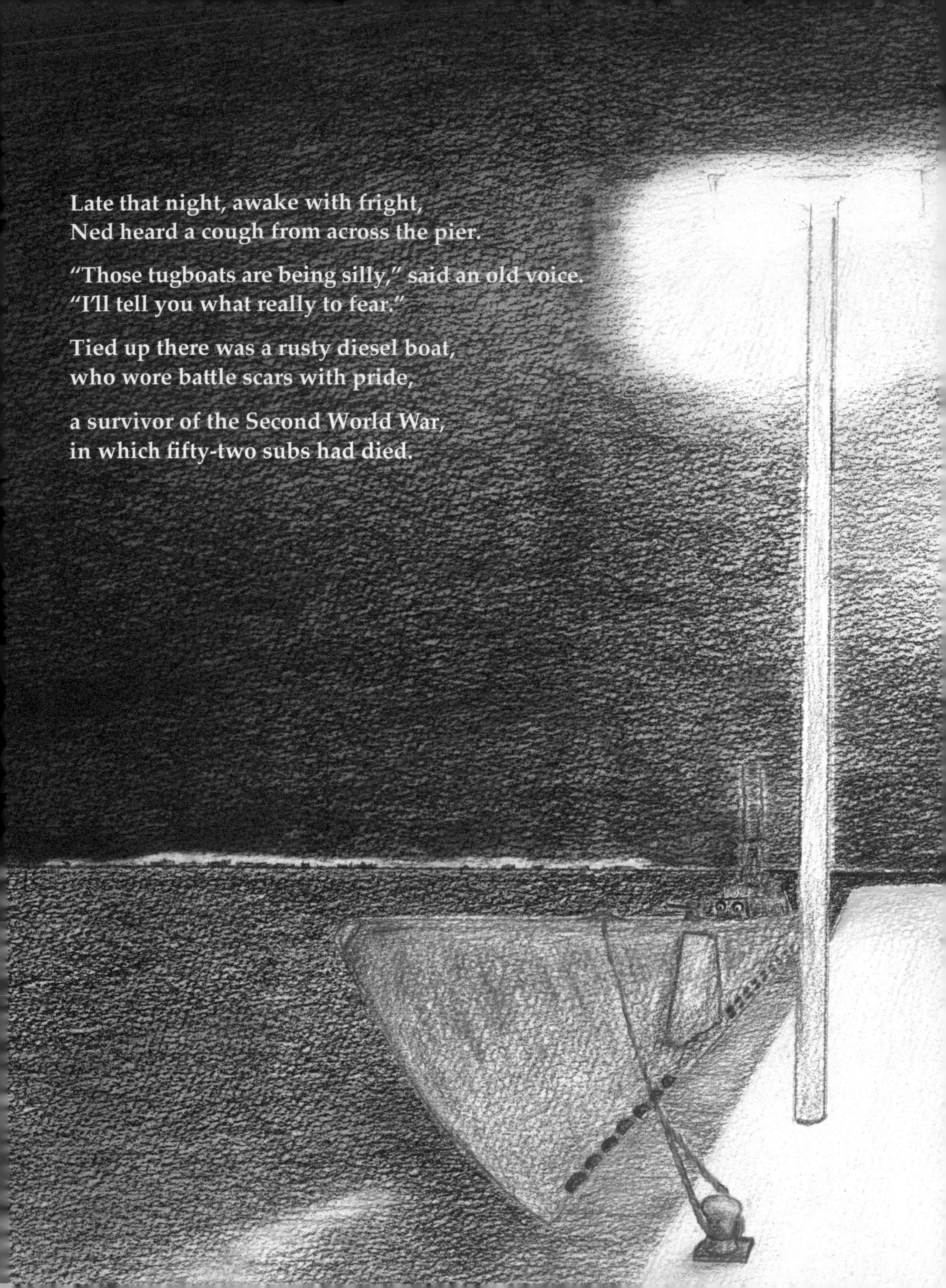

Late that night, awake with fright,
Ned heard a cough from across the pier.

"Those tugboats are being silly," said an old voice.
"I'll tell you what really to fear."

Tied up there was a rusty diesel boat,
who wore battle scars with pride,

a survivor of the Second World War,
in which fifty-two subs had died.

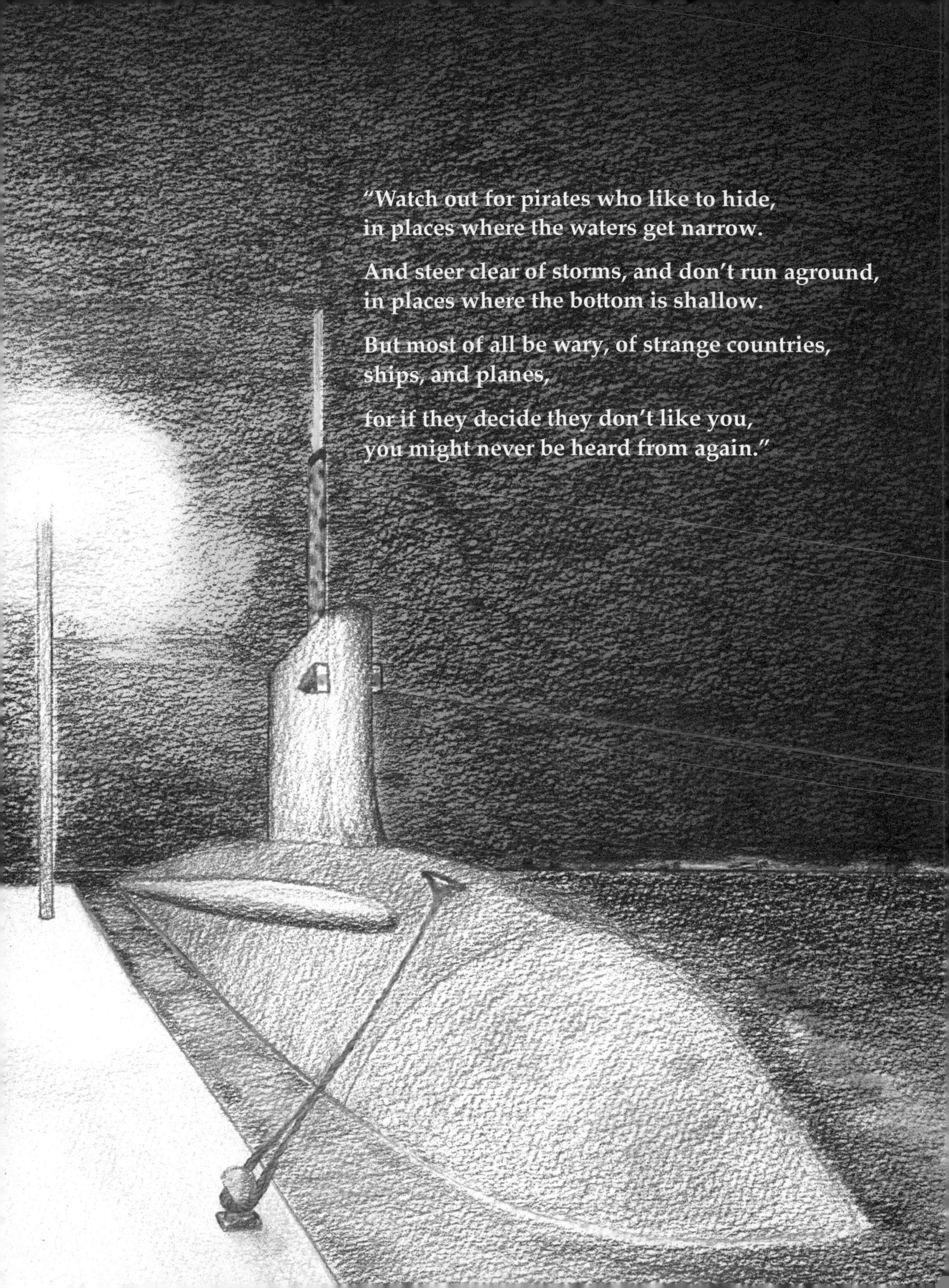

"Watch out for pirates who like to hide,
in places where the waters get narrow.

And steer clear of storms, and don't run aground,
in places where the bottom is shallow.

But most of all be wary, of strange countries,
ships, and planes,

for if they decide they don't like you,
you might never be heard from again."

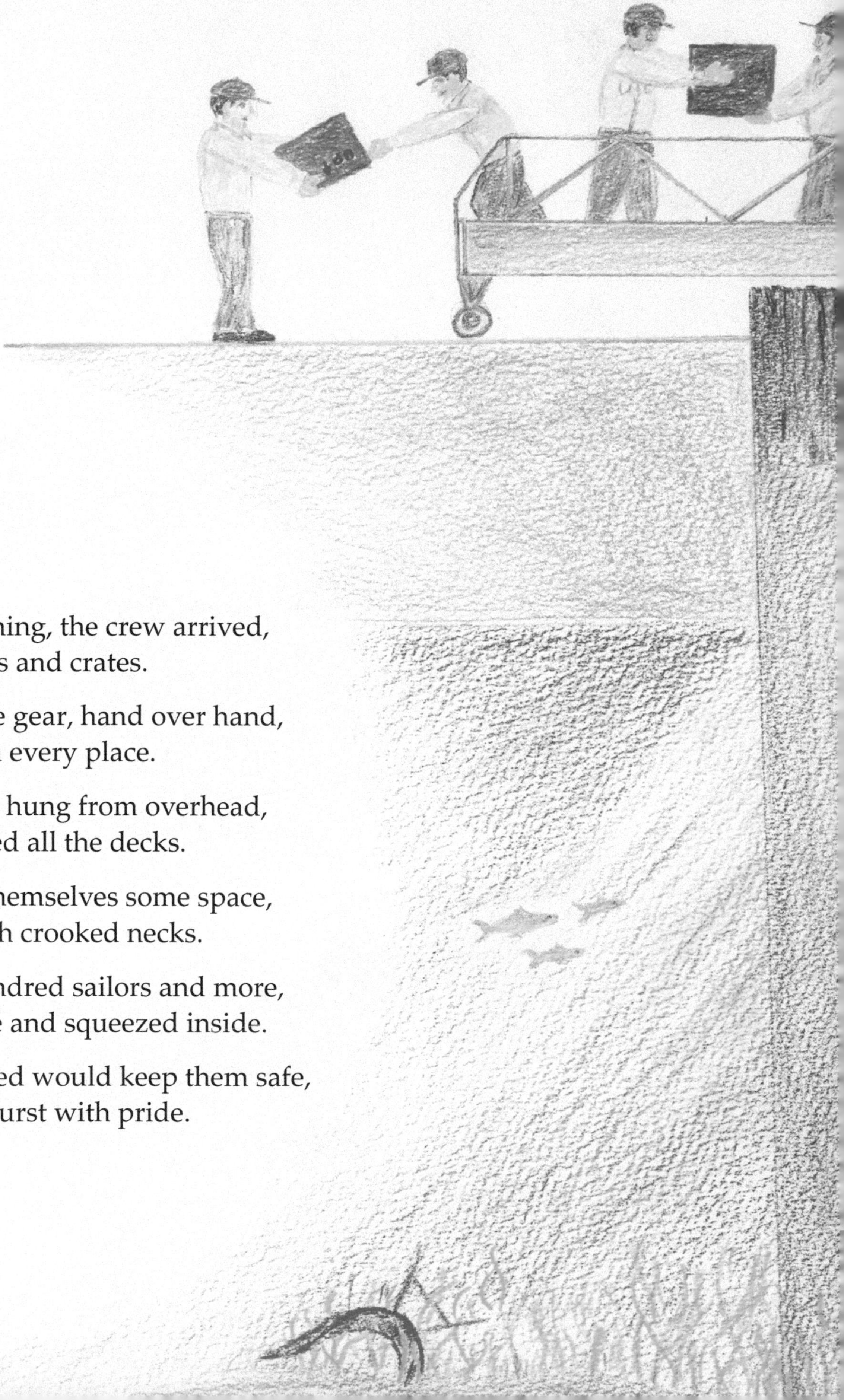

Early next morning, the crew arrived,
with boxes, cans and crates.

They loaded the gear, hand over hand,
and stuffed it in every place.

Some food they hung from overhead,
and cans covered all the decks.

Until they ate themselves some space,
they'd walk with crooked necks.

Somehow a hundred sailors and more,
waved goodbye and squeezed inside.

They trusted Ned would keep them safe,
and he nearly burst with pride.

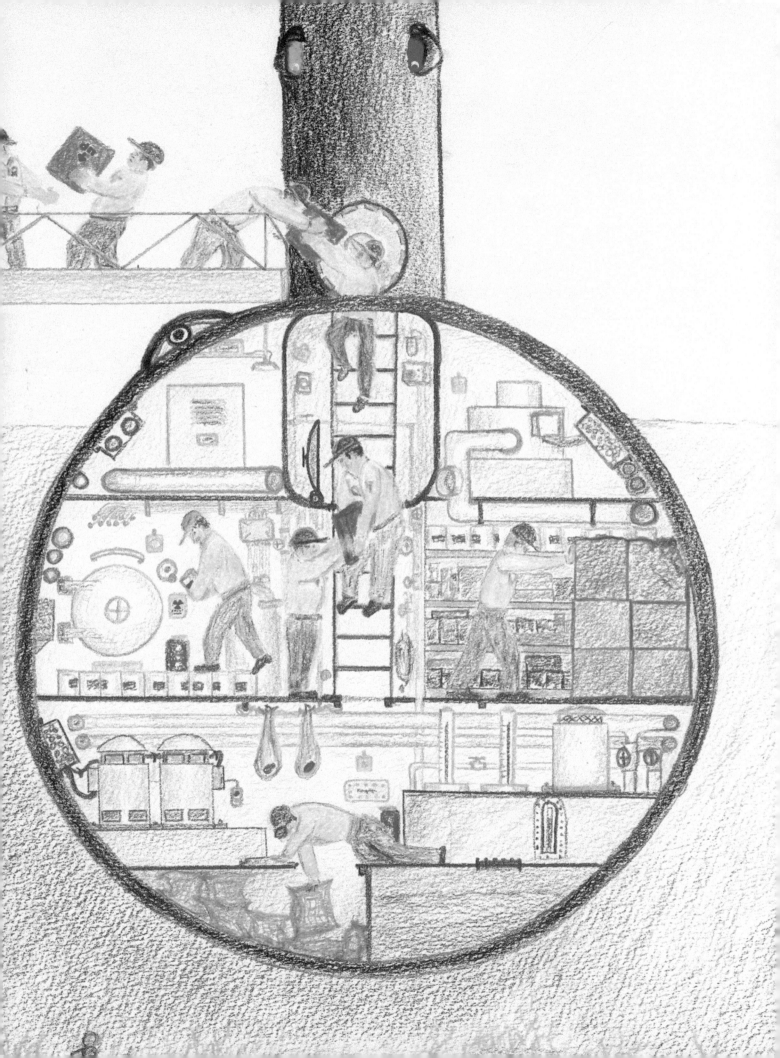

But now the time had come at last, to start a voyage long and fast,
that would take them 'round the world.

So sailors operating the reactor core, withdrew control rods more and more,
that let neutrons start to swirl.

On the uranium fuel, the neutrons beat,
splitting the atoms and releasing the heat, which turned water into steam.

Super hot high-pressure gas, the steam hit turbines with a blast,
causing them to spin real fast—the power-making machines.

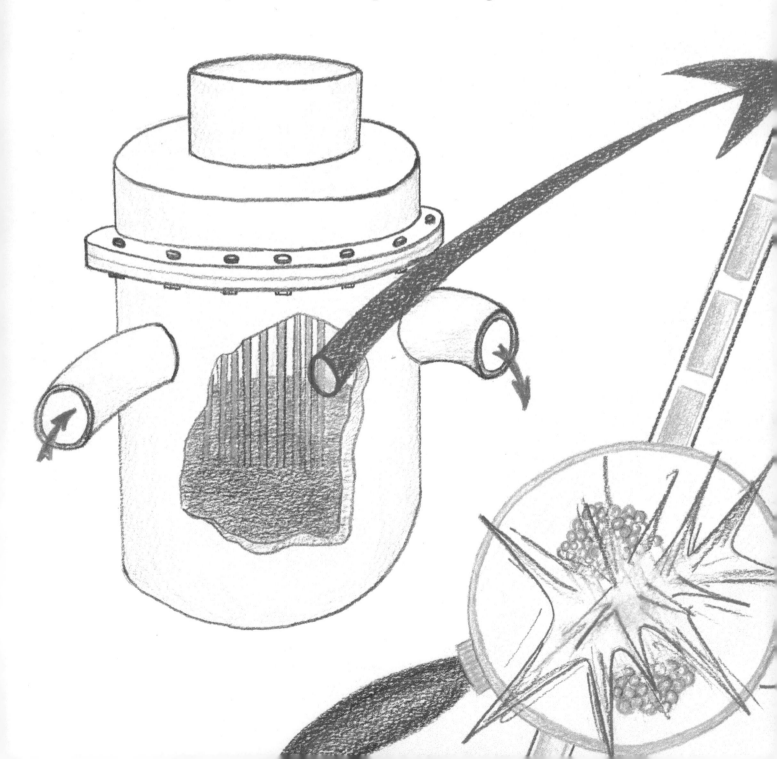

The shaft turned the gears, which in turn drove the screw,
while magnets made power for lights and air too,
by zapping seawater into three parts.

One part oxygen, for the crew to breathe, and two parts hydrogen,
which they didn't need, so out it's pumped in a steady bleed—
like little submarine farts.

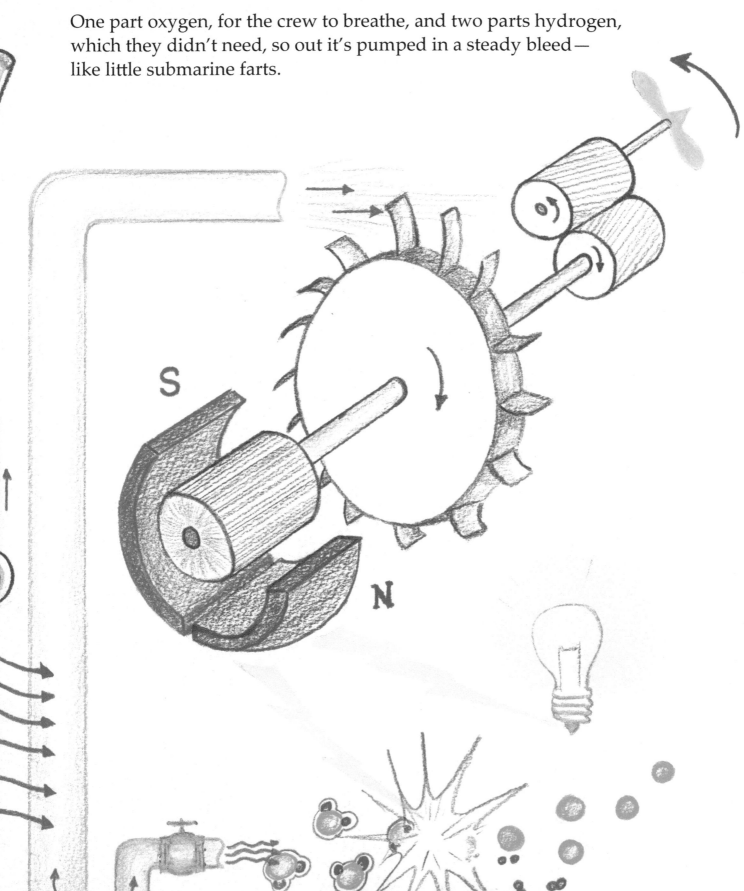

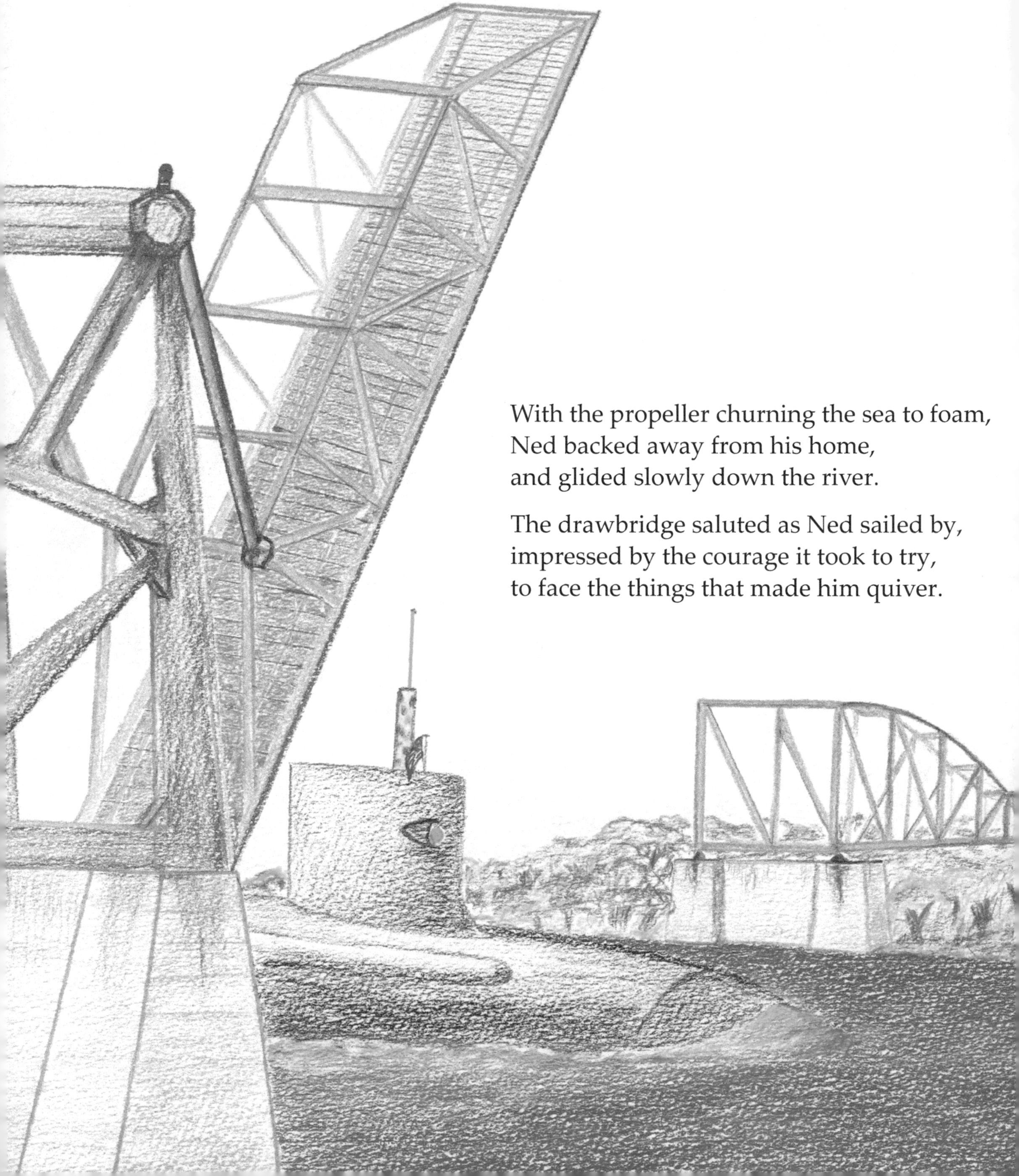

With the propeller churning the sea to foam,
Ned backed away from his home,
and glided slowly down the river.

The drawbridge saluted as Ned sailed by,
impressed by the courage it took to try,
to face the things that made him quiver.

Past the little red lighthouse on the rocks,
Ned's flag waved to the kids waving on the docks,
and he tried to look as brave as he could be.

How the adventure might end, there was no way to know,
but a first step was a necessary start and so,
he stayed true to his course, and quietly put out to sea.

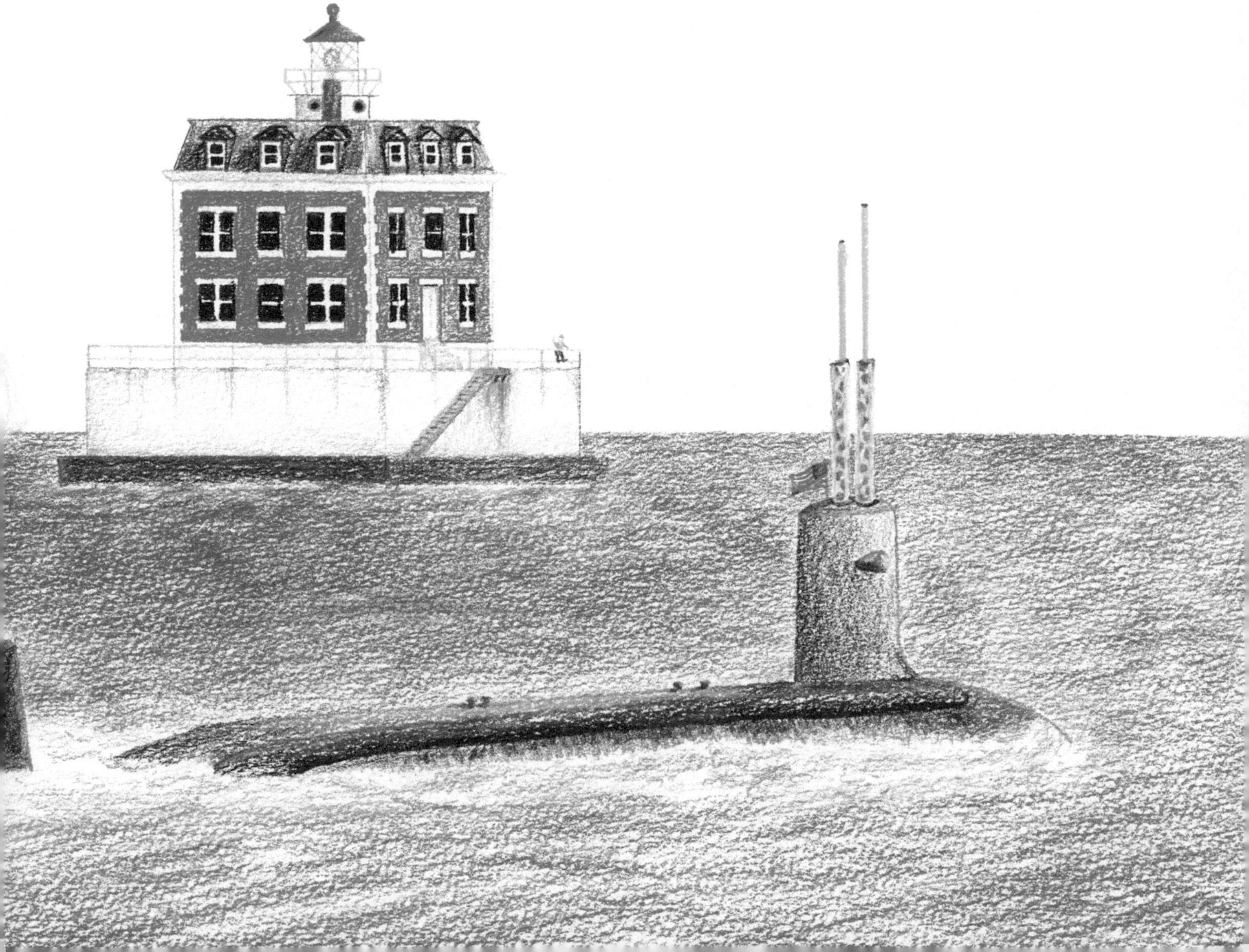

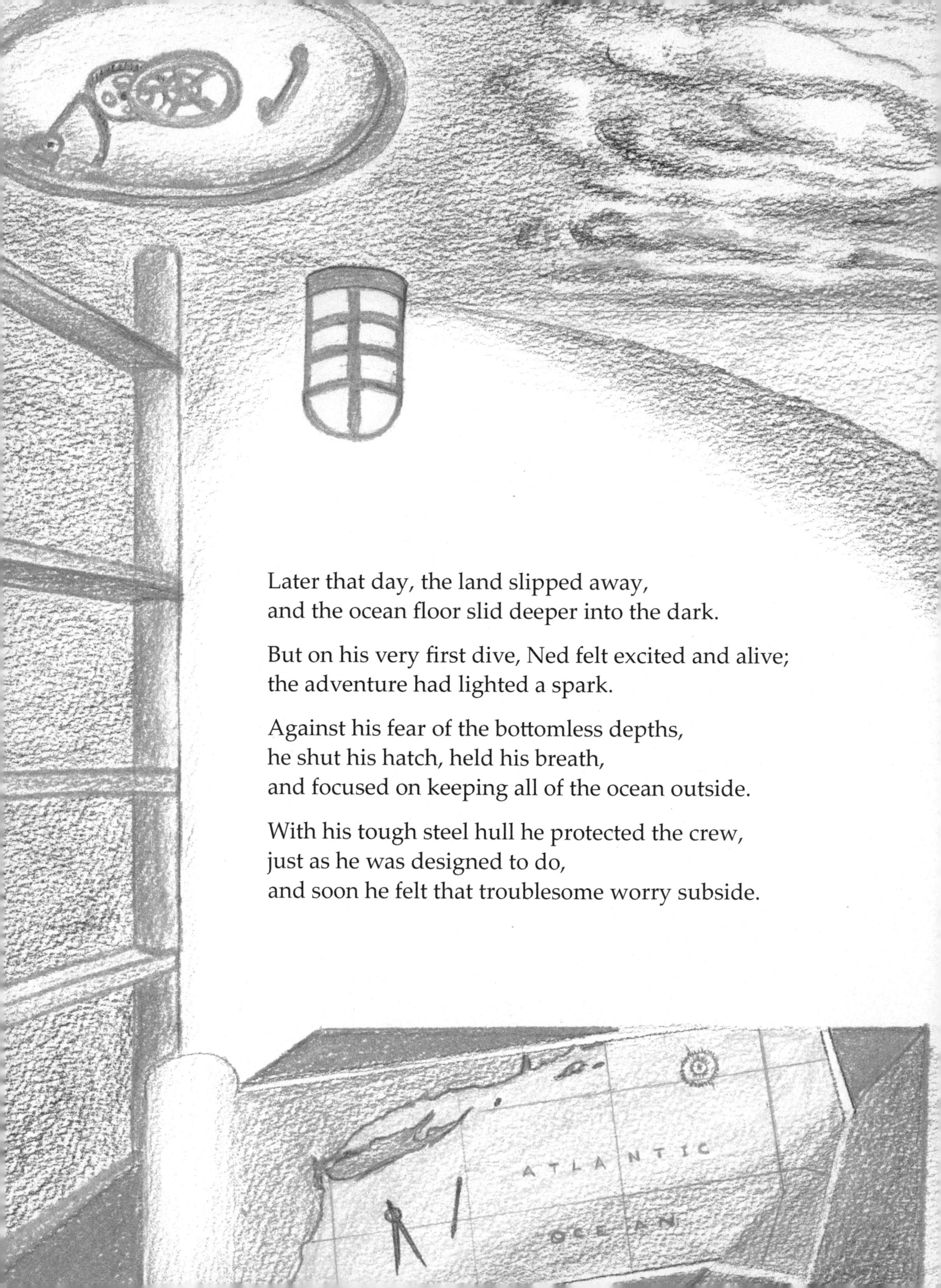
ATLANTIC
OCEAN

Later that day, the land slipped away,
and the ocean floor slid deeper into the dark.

But on his very first dive, Ned felt excited and alive;
the adventure had lighted a spark.

Against his fear of the bottomless depths,
he shut his hatch, held his breath,
and focused on keeping all of the ocean outside.

With his tough steel hull he protected the crew,
just as he was designed to do,
and soon he felt that troublesome worry subside.

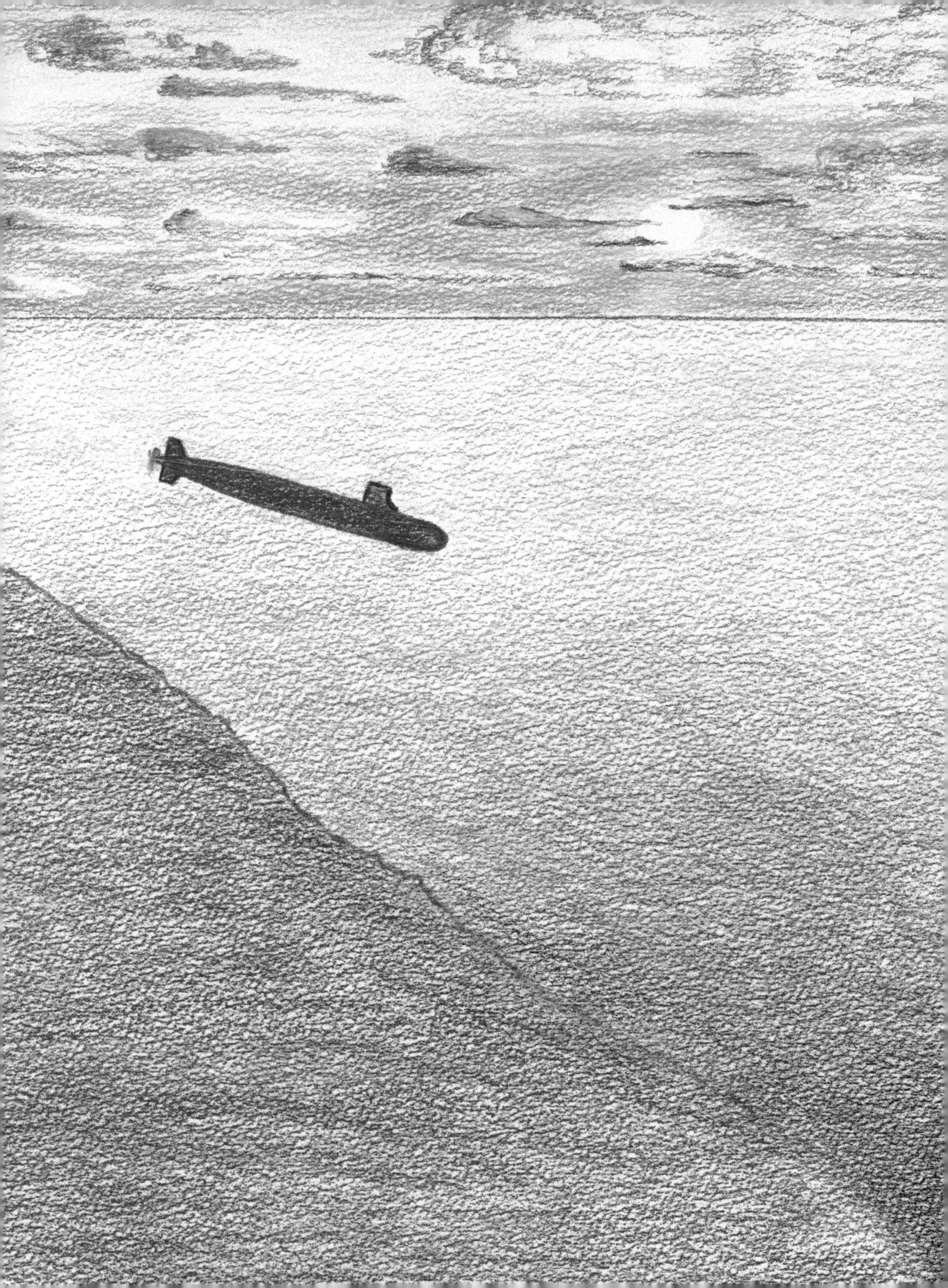

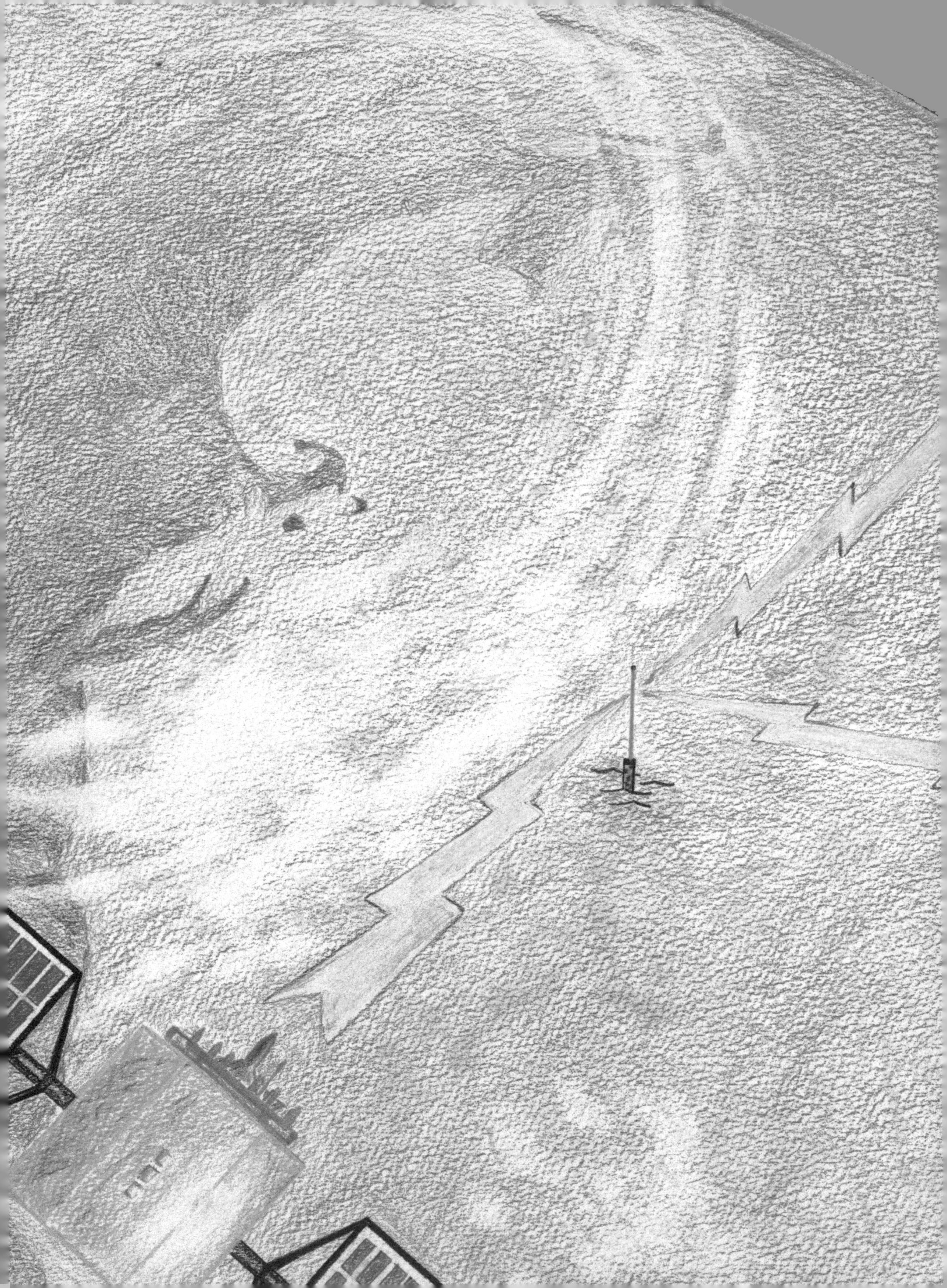

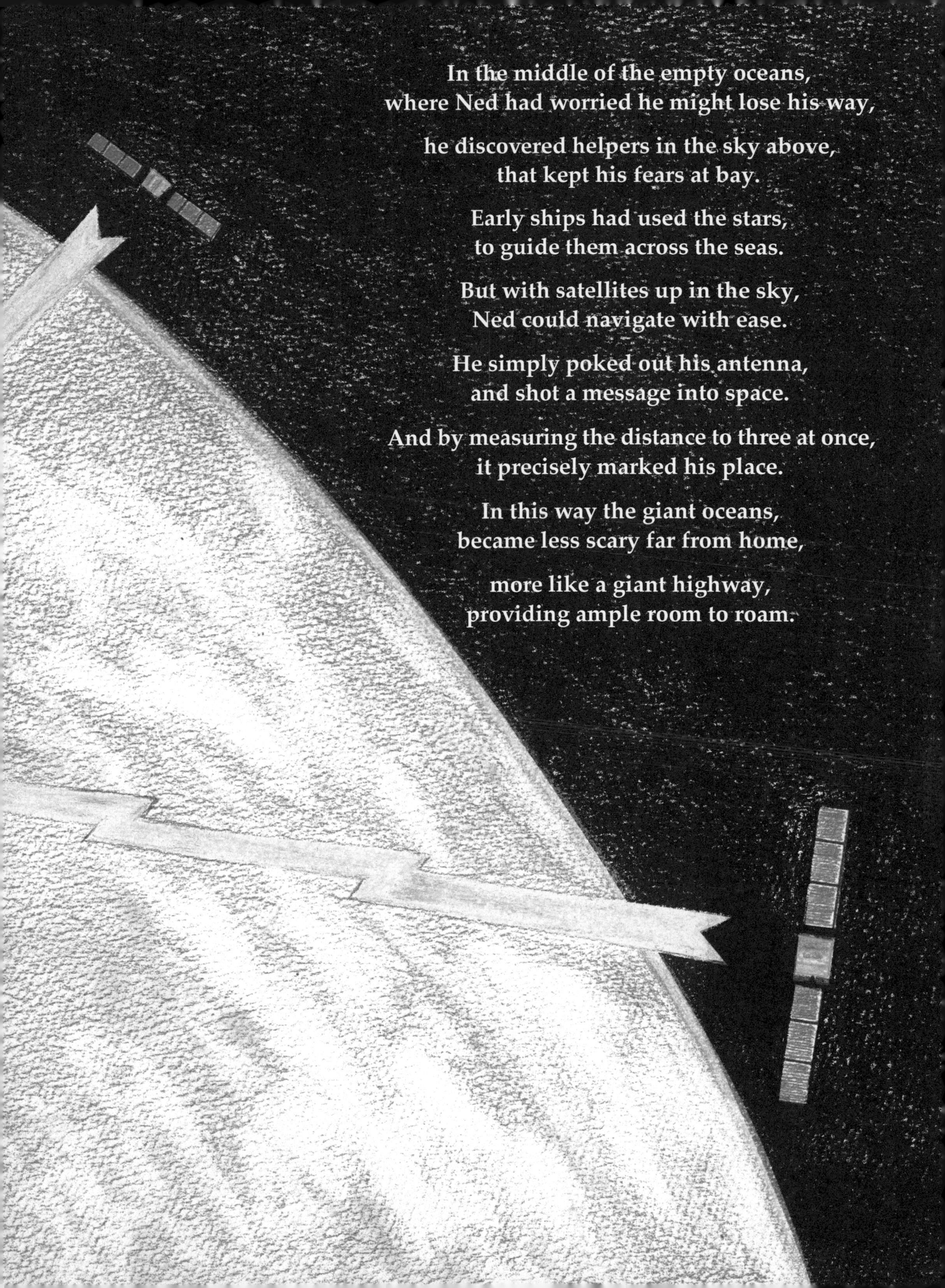

In the middle of the empty oceans,
where Ned had worried he might lose his way,

he discovered helpers in the sky above,
that kept his fears at bay.

Early ships had used the stars,
to guide them across the seas.

But with satellites up in the sky,
Ned could navigate with ease.

He simply poked out his antenna,
and shot a message into space.

And by measuring the distance to three at once,
it precisely marked his place.

In this way the giant oceans,
became less scary far from home,

more like a giant highway,
providing ample room to roam.

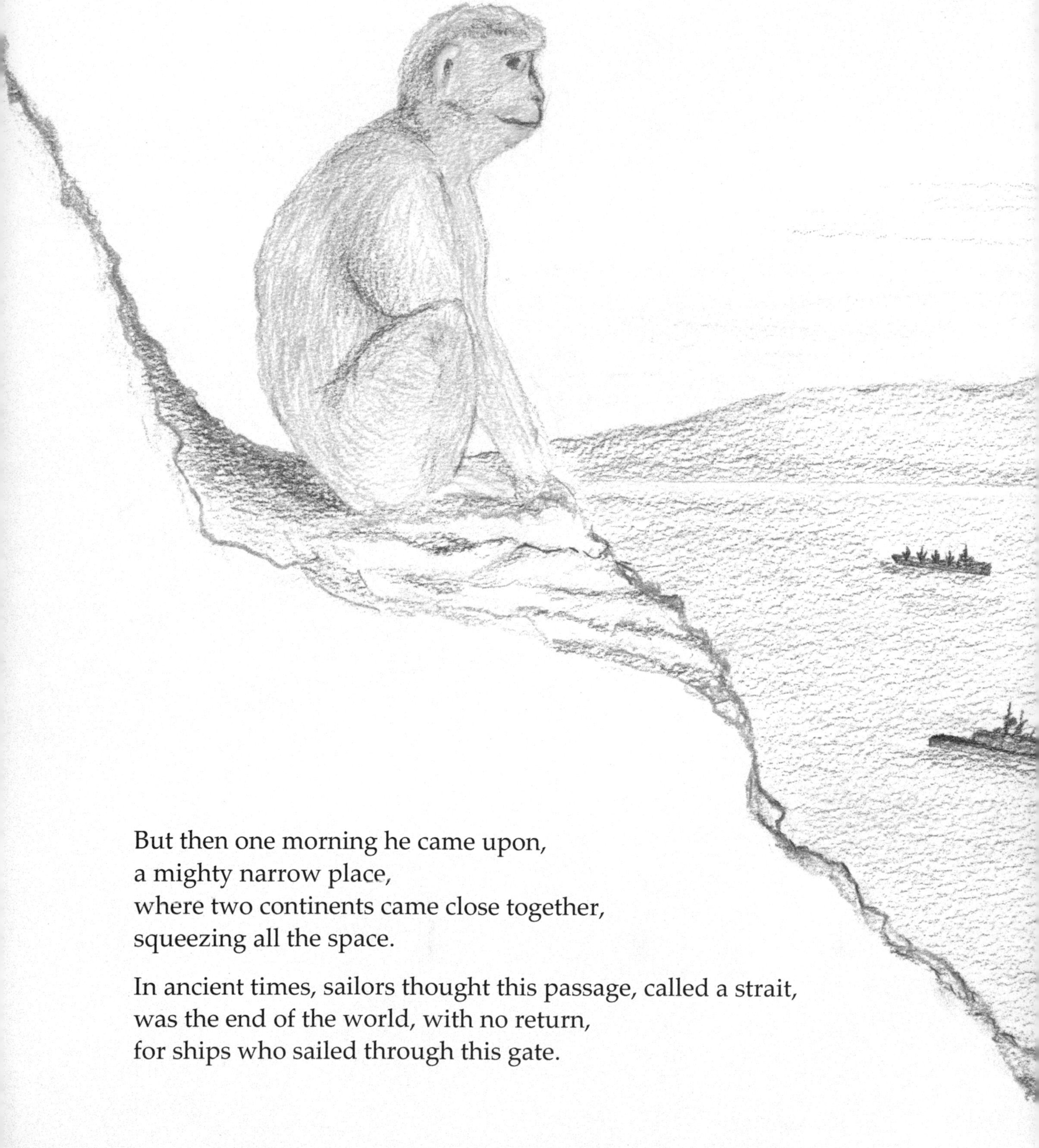

But then one morning he came upon,
a mighty narrow place,
where two continents came close together,
squeezing all the space.

In ancient times, sailors thought this passage, called a strait,
was the end of the world, with no return,
for ships who sailed through this gate.

But Ned didn't have the time, to fear the silly tale,
with all the shipping traffic, he had to watch just where he sailed.

For this was not the edge, where the earth fell into space,
but an important route for trade, and a very busy place.

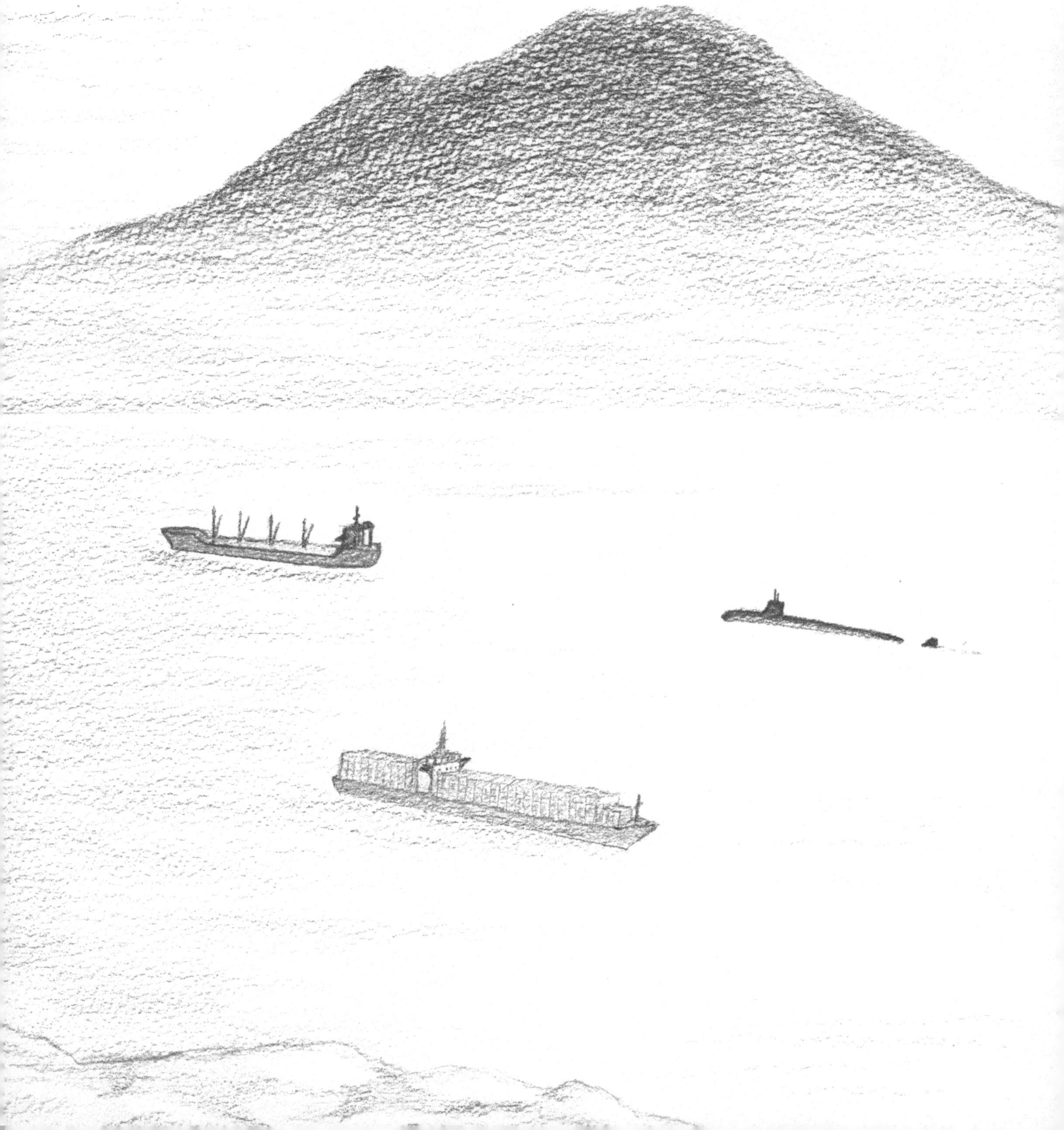

Periscope up, to take in the sights,
ships steam by day, and planes twinkle at night,

but none are an enemy seeking a fight,
or a pirate ship out to inspire much fright.

Instead, an islander in an outrigger canoe,
is staring in wonder right back at you.

Modern and old, suddenly meet,
and both find the discovery, quite a treat,
inspiring a new point of view.

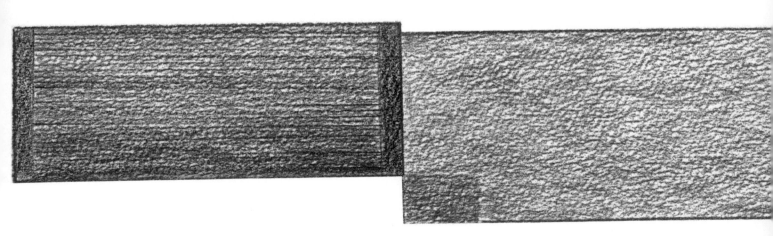

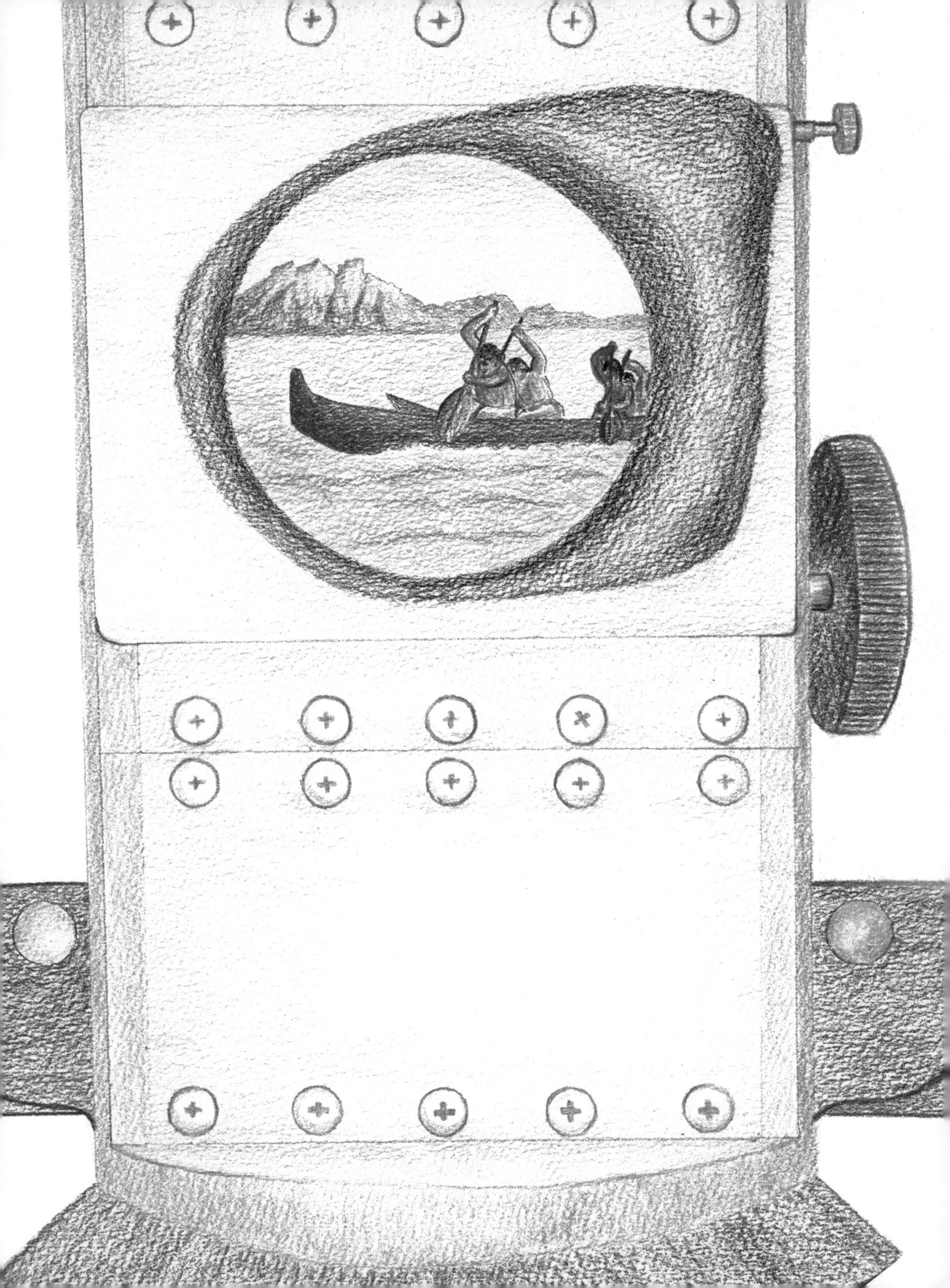

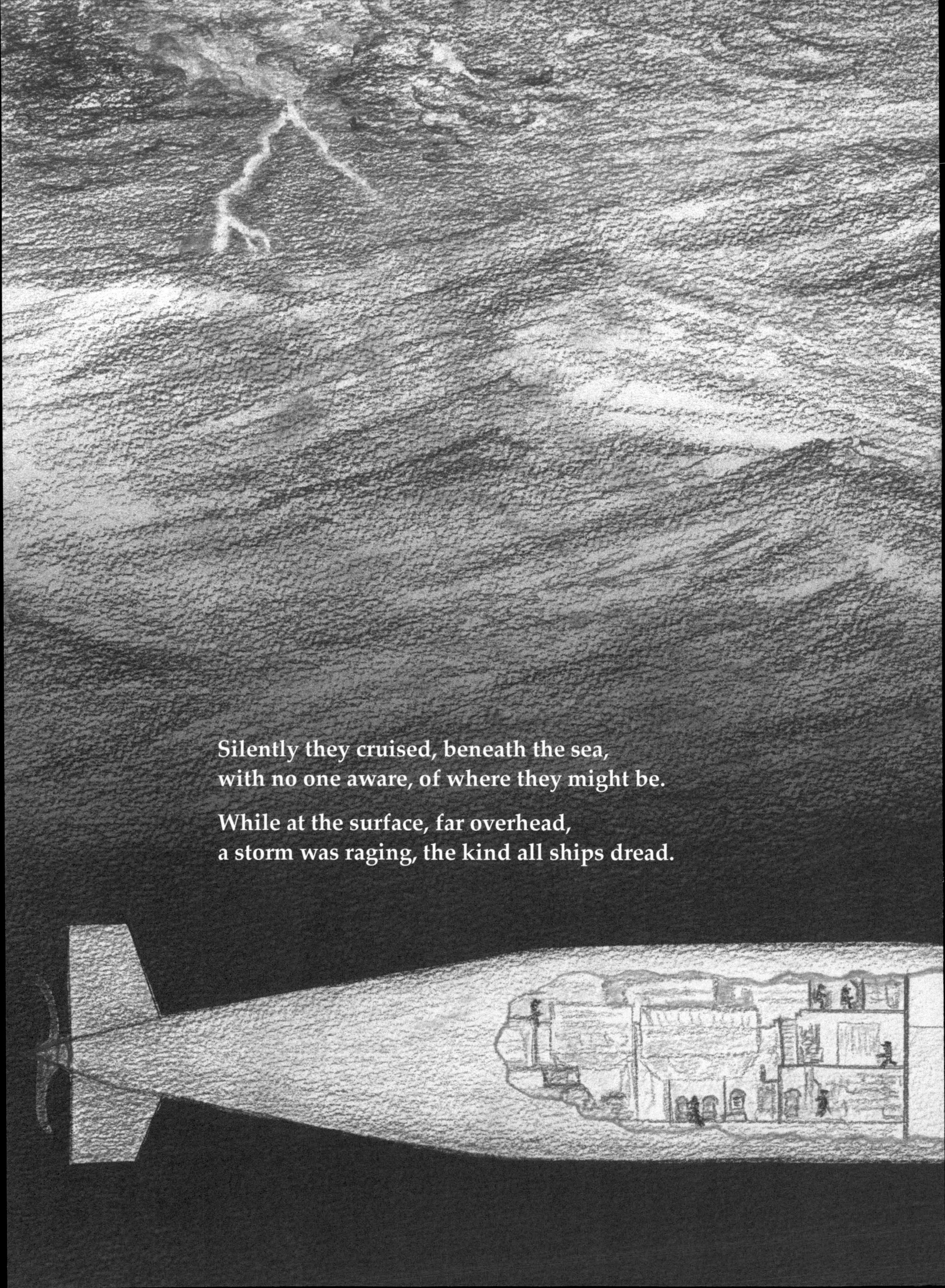

Silently they cruised, beneath the sea,
with no one aware, of where they might be.

While at the surface, far overhead,
a storm was raging, the kind all ships dread.

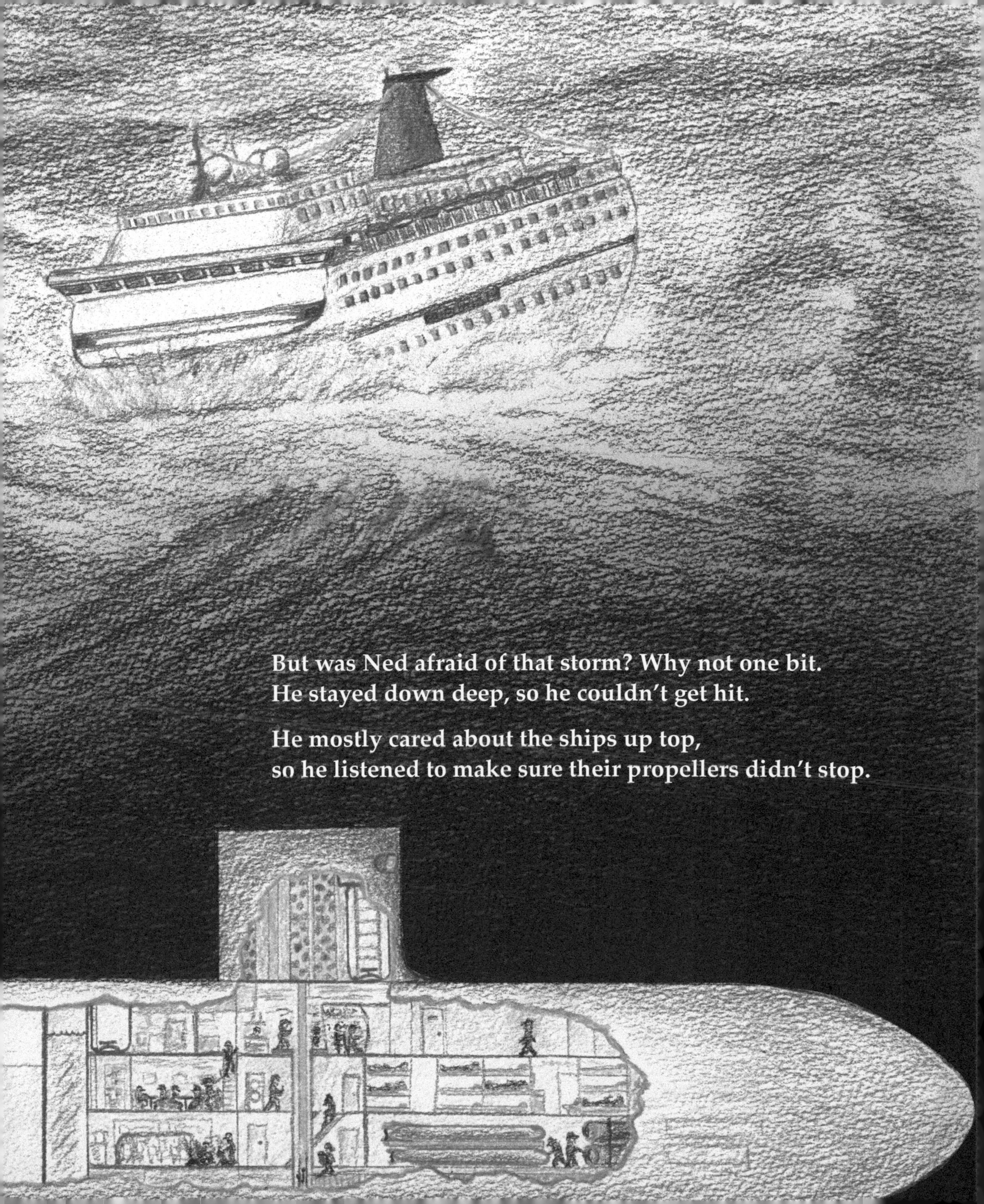

But was Ned afraid of that storm? Why not one bit.
He stayed down deep, so he couldn't get hit.

He mostly cared about the ships up top,
so he listened to make sure their propellers didn't stop.

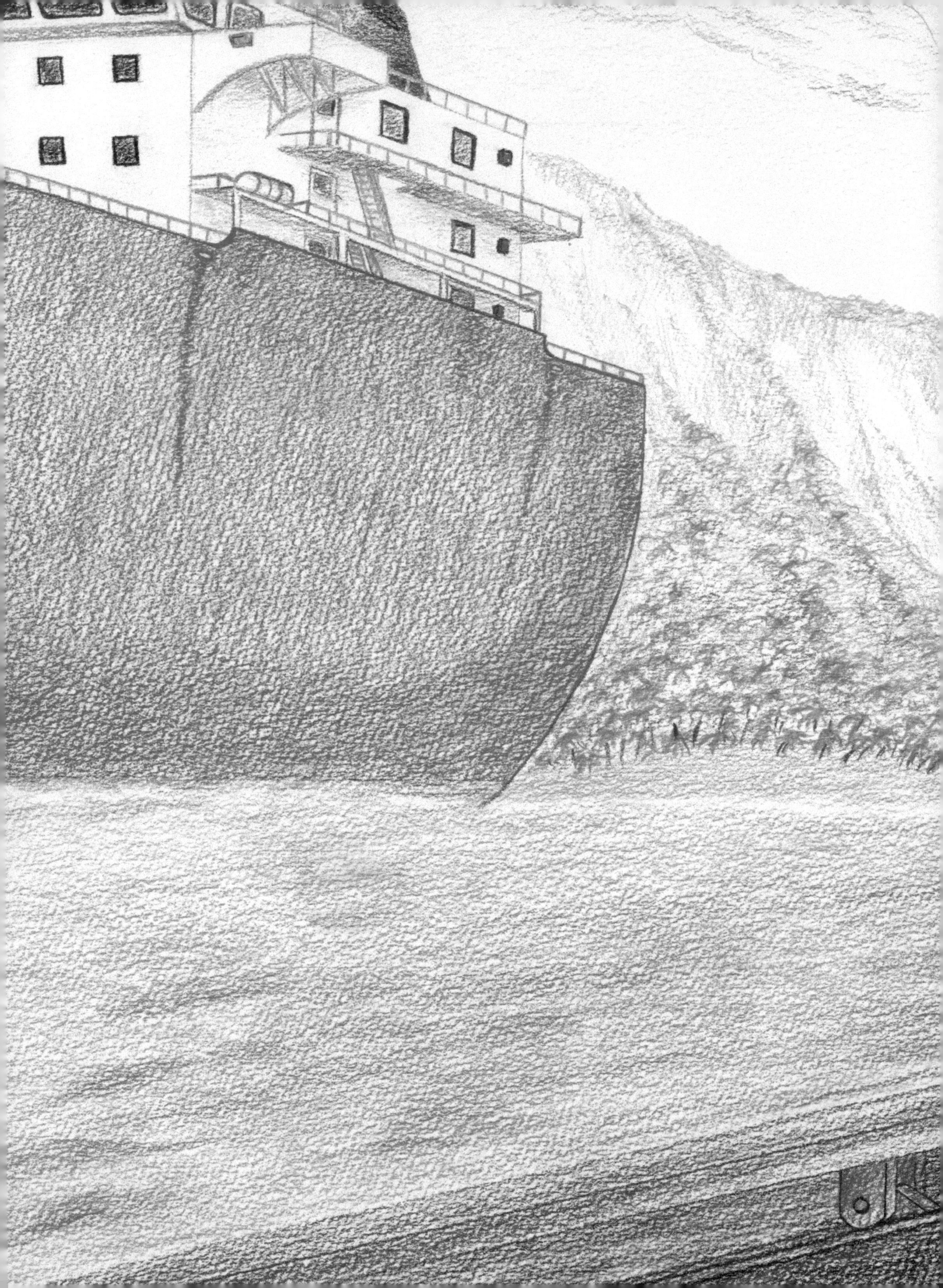

Each day he sailed a little more, building distance from home shores,
exploring lands far-flung.

Weird smells and strange sights, foreign cultures brought delight,
and the sound of unusual tongues.

So much to learn, so much to do, Ned had no time to be afraid too,
and so he just had fun.

Dodging giant container ships, 'round sailing boats making fishing trips,
he ran as far as he could run.

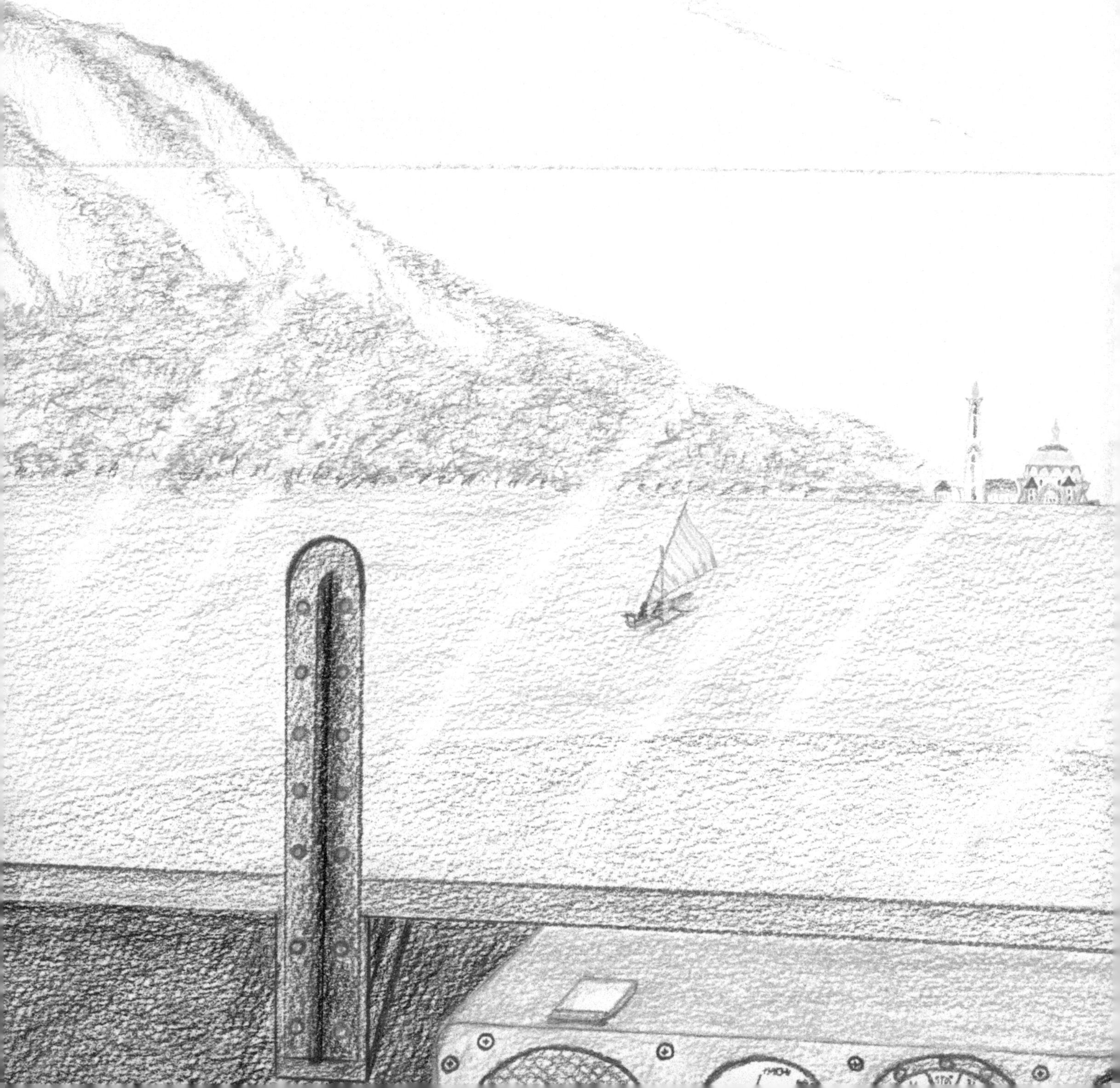

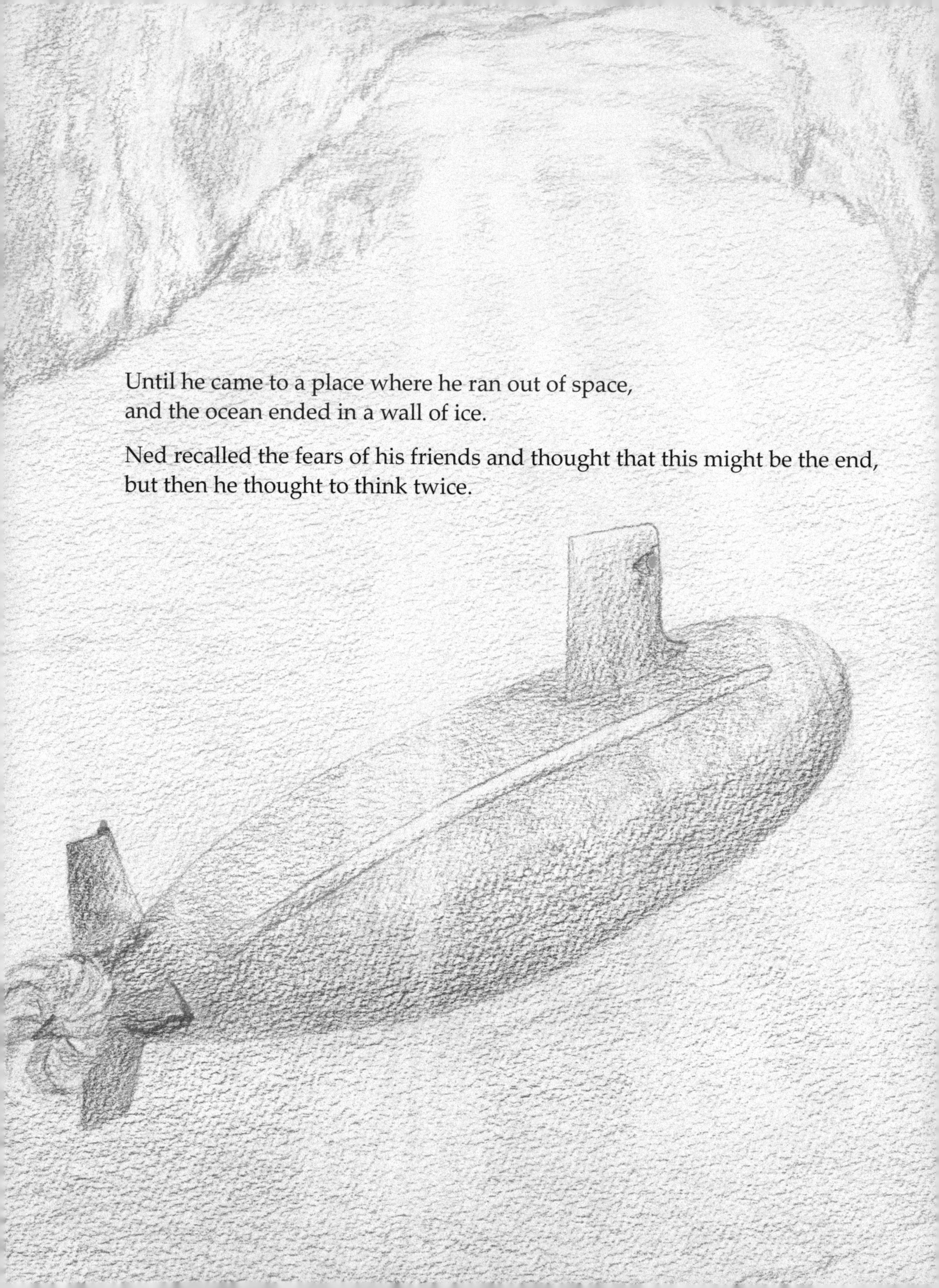

Until he came to a place where he ran out of space,
and the ocean ended in a wall of ice.

Ned recalled the fears of his friends and thought that this might be the end,
but then he thought to think twice.

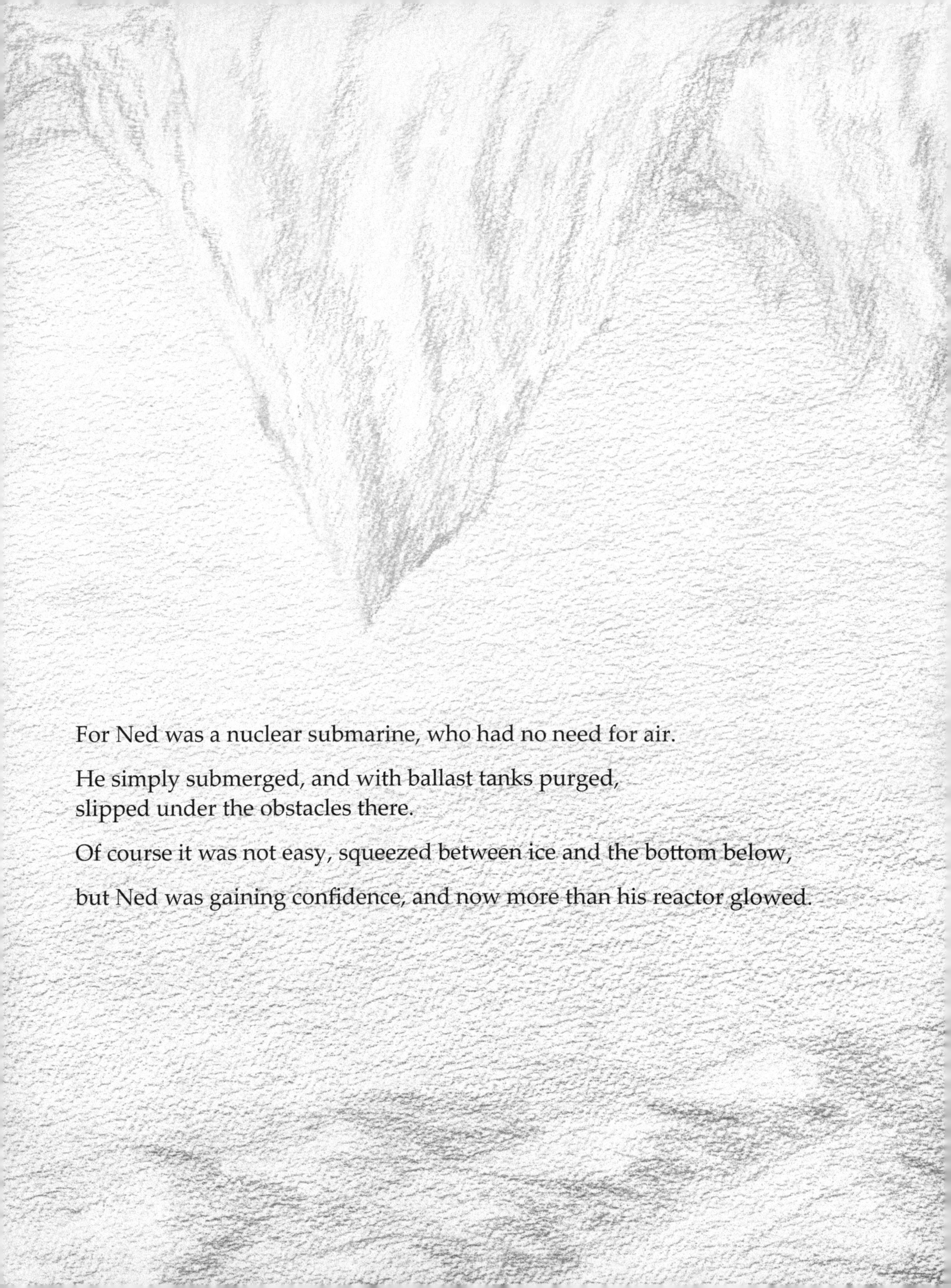

For Ned was a nuclear submarine, who had no need for air.

He simply submerged, and with ballast tanks purged,
slipped under the obstacles there.

Of course it was not easy, squeezed between ice and the bottom below,

but Ned was gaining confidence, and now more than his reactor glowed.

At the top of the world, he felt on top of his game,
and needed someplace to shout it.

But the only way out, was through ice rather stout,
and so for a moment he doubted.

Once more he summoned courage, and also a lot of air.
Blowing his tanks, he rammed the ice bank,
and suddenly found himself up there.

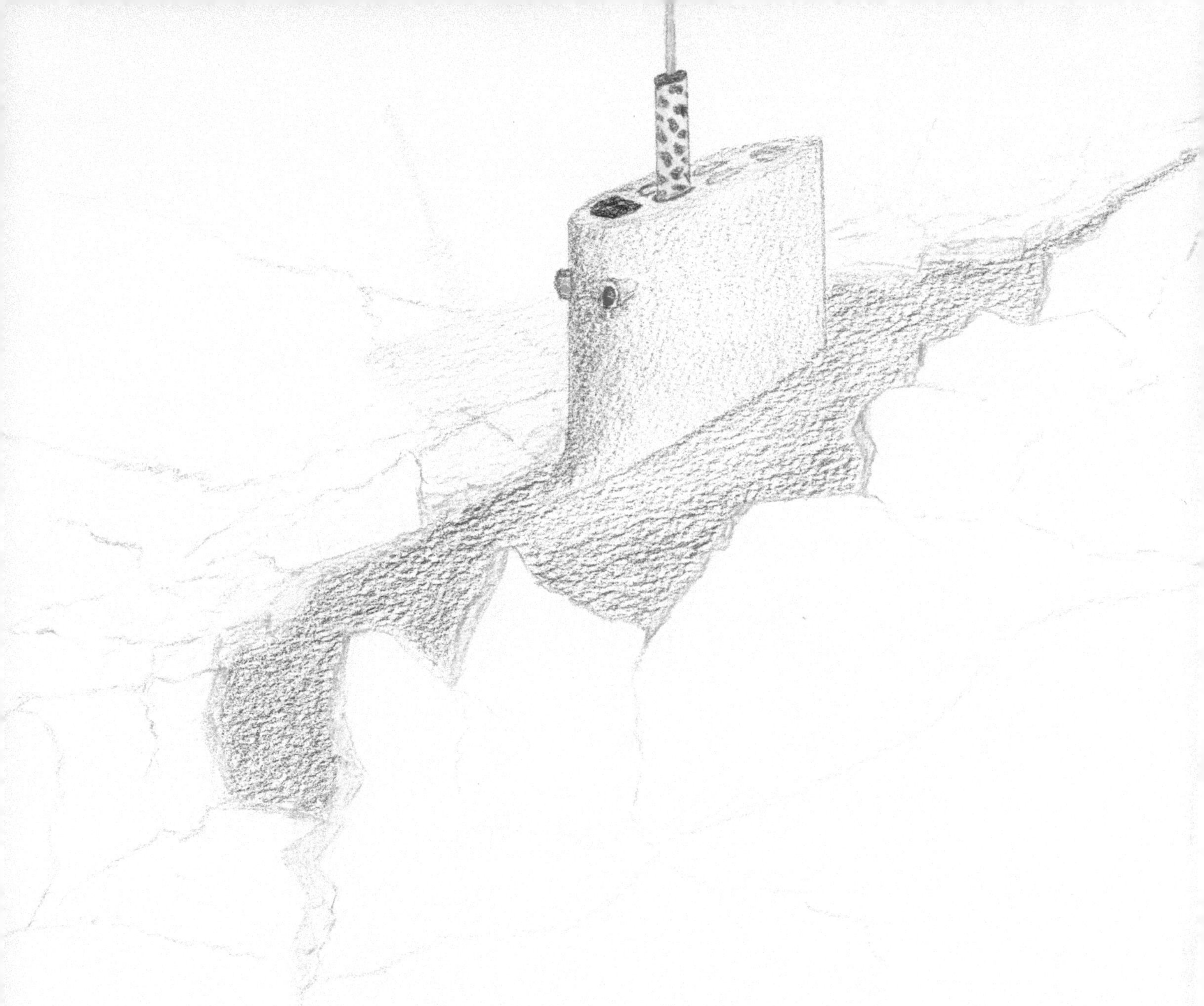

To his surprise, before his eyes,
were creatures on the ice.

Not sea monsters but polar bears,
which Ned thought seemed kind of nice.

He told them of all the things he'd seen,
and how he had conquered his fear.

But when they discovered he was not a real meal,
they left to find seals or reindeer.

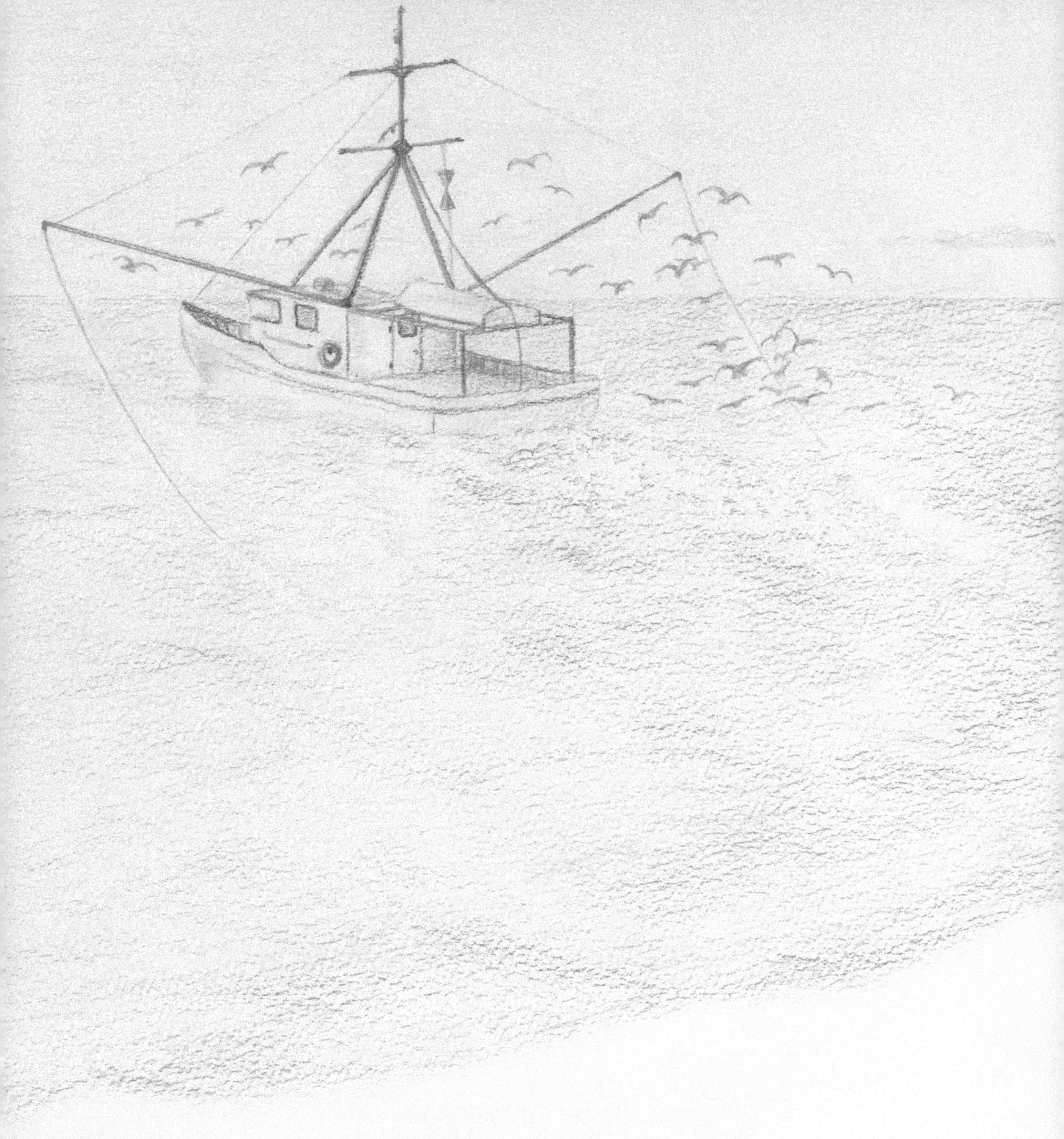

From this spot on the globe, every place lay south,
so south was his course home.

And when the fishing fleet hove into view, he kicked it up a notch or two,
his periscope flicking up foam.

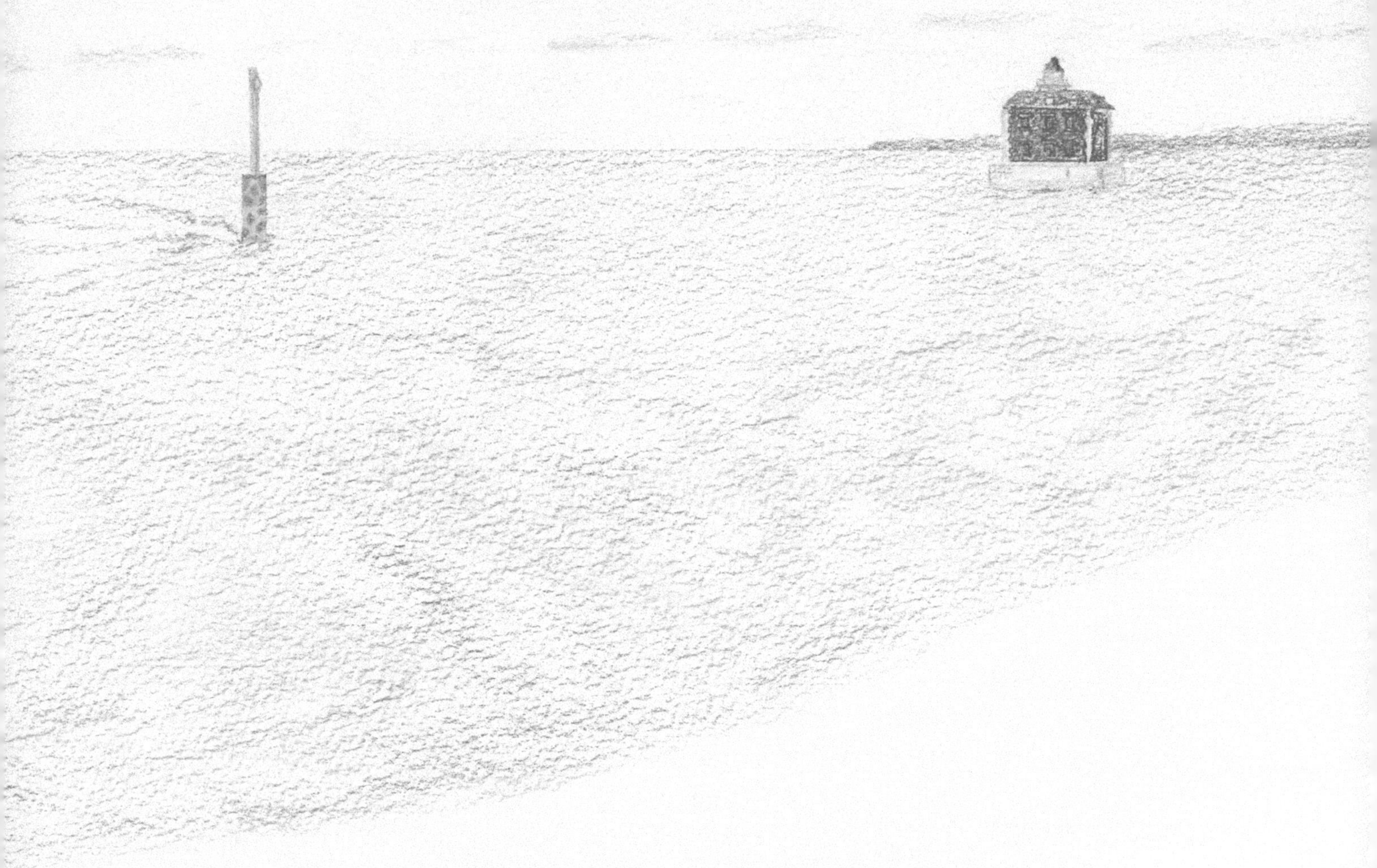

Up the river to his friends, he sailed with a smile,
radiating confidence visible for miles,
and returning with a story that could hardly be believed.

Not merely farther than anyone before,
but as far as one could sail from shore, was the story they received.

Yet still, some remained frozen by worries,
and others, content with what they knew,
for venturing out over the horizon, required courage and ambition too.

But when new subs arrived at base, and tied alongside Ned,
he didn't hide the fears and challenges, but this is what he said:

"Love your home, but fear not to roam, for the world has so much more.
Ships are safe in harbors, but that's not what ships are for."*

Historical Endnotes

Launching USS *Nautilus*

USS *Nautilus* was the world's first nuclear power submarine. Built by the Electric Boat Company in Groton, Connecticut, she was launched into the Thames River on January 21, 1954. A year later she put to sea for the first time, signaling her historic message: "Underway on nuclear power." In 1958, under the command of Commander William R. Anderson, she became the first vessel to make a submerged transit of the North Pole. Among the most difficult parts of the mission—named Operation Sunshine—was navigating the shallow water of the Bering Strait, where the ice extended as much as sixty feet below sea level. It required two attempts to successfully pass into the Arctic Ocean. This and other voyages of USS *Nautilus* are featured in *The Ice Diaries: The Untold Story of the Cold War's Most Daring Mission* by William Anderson and Don Keith.

USS *Skate* at the North Pole

USS *Skate* was America's third nuclear submarine, and the first to surface at the North Pole while under the command of Commander James Calvert. Operating out of the submarine base in New London, Connecticut, she made several forays into the Arctic, first surfacing at the pole on March 17, 1959, and then again in the company of USS *Seadragon* from the Pacific Fleet on August 2, 1962. The crew planted an American flag, built a cairn of ice blocks to commemorate the event and committed the ashes of the late Arctic explorer Sir Hubert Wilkens. The adventures are captured in the book *Surface at the Pole: The Extraordinary Voyages of the* USS *Skate* by James Calvert.

USS *Triton*

USS *Triton* was launched in 1958, the only United States submarine to be equipped with two nuclear reactors. Under the command of Captain Edward L. Beach, Jr., her first assignment was Operation Sandblast, a submerged circumnavigation of the earth. Over the course of sixty days and twenty-one hours she sailed 26,723 nautical miles westward following the same track as the first circumnavigation in 1521 led by Ferdinand Magellan. She remained virtually undetected except during her transit of the Philippine Islands when her periscope was spotted on April Fool's Day by a local man paddling a dugout canoe. Read about it in *Around the World Submerged: The Voyage of the Triton* by Edward Beach.

Captain Beach in USS *Triton*

Captain Edward Beach was a highly decorated officer having made twelve submarine combat patrols during World War II, including one in USS *Tirante* that earned him the Navy Cross and his captain the Medal of Honor. He served as Naval Aide to President Eisenhower and published thirteen books, of which *Run Silent Run Deep* is best known. His nickname was "Ned."

*The expression by Ned that appears as the last line of this book is a commonly held sentiment within the sea services. This quotation is most often attributed to John A. Shedd.

CPSIA information can be obtained
at www.ICGtesting.com
Printed in the USA
LVHW071220230119
604884LV00003B/15/P

9 781633 372399